This Little Tiger book belongs to:

_____

_____

_____

For Rala – P. B.

To Chris, Sally, Maya and Gabriel – J. C.

LITTLE TIGER PRESS LTD,
an imprint of the Little Tiger Group
1 The Coda Centre, 189 Munster Road, London SW6 6AW
www.littletiger.co.uk

First published in Great Britain 2011
This edition published 2017
Text copyright © Paul Bright 2011
Illustrations copyright © Jane Chapman 2011
Visit Jane Chapman at www.ChapmanandWarnes.com
Paul Bright and Jane Chapman have asserted their rights to be
identified as the author and illustrator of this work
under the Copyright, Designs and Patents Act, 1988

ISBN 978-1-84869-806-2
Printed in China • LTP/1800/1895/0717

2 4 6 8 10 9 7 5 3 1

The Not-So Scary Snorklum

by Paul Bright

Illustrated by Jane Chapman

LITTLE TIGER

LONDON

The setting sun glowed orange as the scary Snorklum stomped home to his cave. "I'm late!" he thought, and his whiskers began to wibble in a worried sort of way.

Then he met Mole. His head told him he was late, but his tummy told him he was hungry.

"I AM THE SCARY SNORKLUM," he growled, "and I am going to have a Mole sandwich."

"If you are the scary Snorklum," said
Mole, "why are your whiskers wibbling
in a worried sort of way?"

"Whiskers wibbling?" snorted the
Snorklum. "Nothing worries a Snorklum!"

He put Mole in his pocket to eat
later and hurried on his way.

The sinking sun glowed red.
"I **must** be home by dark,"
muttered the Snorklum, and his tail began
to **twitch** in a timid sort of way.

Then he met Rabbit. His head told him he was very late, but his tummy told him that a Rabbit pie would be even better than a Mole sandwich.

"I AM THE SCARY SNORKLUM,"

he snarled, "and I am going to have Rabbit pie."

"If you are the scary Snorklum," said Rabbit, "why is your tail twitching in a timid sort of way?"

"Tail twitching?" snorted the Snorklum. "Timid? Oh, no. Snorklums aren't timid. They're scary—really scary."

He put Rabbit in his bag to eat later and hurried on.

The sun dipped and disappeared.
"I **must** be home by nighttime!"
gasped the Snorklum. And his knees
began to **knock** in a nervous sort
of way.

Then he met Badger.

His head told him that he was **very**, very
late, but his tummy told him that Badger stew
would be even tastier than Rabbit pie.

"I AM THE SCARY SNORKLUM,"

he roared, "and I am going to make some
Badger stew."

"If you really are the scary Snorklum," said Badger,
"why are your knees knocking?"

"And your tail twitching?" said Rabbit.

"And your whiskers wibbling?" added Mole.

"Are you a scary Snorklum or . . .

a scared Snorklum?"

"Or maybe," said Badger, "you're
not a Snorklum at all!"

"Of course I am a Snorklum!" bellowed the
Snorklum, quite forgetting that he was in a hurry.
"I can prove it! And when I'm done . . .

I WILL EAT ALL OF YOU FOR SUPPER!"

"I have heard," said Badger, "that a scary Snorklum can **scare the leaves** off the trees with a single stare."

"**I can do that**," said the Snorklum. He screwed up his face and he stared.

The trees shook and shivered,

and their leaves fluttered

to the ground.

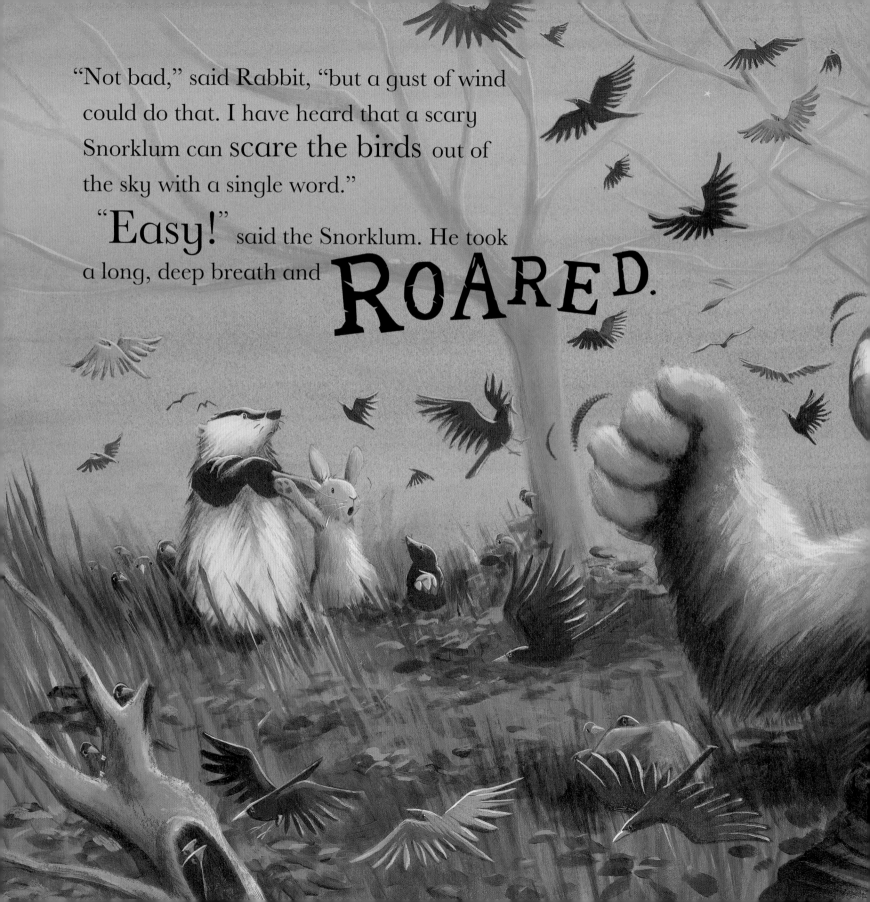

"Not bad," said Rabbit, "but a gust of wind
could do that. I have heard that a scary
Snorklum can scare the birds out of
the sky with a single word."

"Easy!" said the Snorklum. He took
a long, deep breath and ROARED.

All the birds flew down
from the sky and hid in the
trees and bushes, trembling.

"But birds settle in trees at night anyway," said Mole. "And you can't be a scary Snorklum, because I have heard that if a scary Snorklum stays out after dark he goes . . ."

As darkness finally fell, the scary Snorklum shrank, with a POOFFT! and a flash and a cry, into a tiny, timid Snorklum.

"You tricked me!" he squeaked.

"But when I've grown big and scary

again, I'll be back! And next time,

I'll have YOU all
for breakfast!"